SQUIDS will be SQUIDS

FRESH MORALS

BEASTLY FABLES

BY JON SCIESZKA & LANE SMITH

DESIGNED BY MOLLY LEACH

PUFFIN BOOKS

FOR ME TO KNOW

— J. S.

FOR YOU TO FIND OUT

— L. S.

the fables

Little Walrus

Elephant & Flea

Termite, Ant, & Echidna

Horseshoe Crab & Blowfish

Piece of Toast & Froot Loops

Slug's Big Moment

Hand, Foot, & Tongue

Duckbilled Platypus vs. BeefSnakStik®

Elephant & Gnat

Gee . . . I Wonder

Fables have been around for thousands of years. And it's no wonder. Because even thousands of years ago people were bright enough to figure out that you could gossip about anybody – as long as you changed their name to something like "Lion" or "Mouse" or "Donkey" first. 〜

Aesop is the person most famous for telling fables. Though he wasn't the first . . . or the best looking. Most descriptions we have of Aesop call him "funny shaped" or "ugly" or worse. But you didn't hear that from me. I think Aesop was a great guy. 〜

Æsop

This book, *Squids Will Be Squids*, is a collection of fables that Aesop might have told if he were alive today and sitting in the back of class daydreaming and goofing around instead of paying attention and correcting his homework like he was supposed to, because his dog ate it and he didn't have time to run out and buy new paper and do it over again before his bus came to pick him up in the morning.

These are beastly fables with fresh morals about all kinds of bossy, sneaky, funny, annoying, dim-bulb people. But nobody I know personally.

Really.

{ **moral**
Sometimes the names are changed to protect the not-so-innocent. }

grasshopper logic

One bright and sunny day, Grasshopper came
home from school, dropped his backpack, and
was just about to run outside to meet his friends.

"Where are you going?" asked his mother.

"Out to meet some friends," said Grasshopper.

"Do you have any homework due tomorrow?" asked his mother.

"Just one small thing for History. I did the rest in class."

"OK," said Mother Grasshopper. "Be back at six for dinner."

Grasshopper hung out with his friends,
came home promptly at six, ate his dinner,
then took out his History homework.

His mother read the assignment and freaked out.

"Rewrite twelve Greek myths as Broadway musicals.
Write music for songs. Design and build all sets.
Sew original costumes for each production."

"How long have
you known about
this assignment?"
she asked,
trying not to scream.

"I don't know," said Grasshopper.

{ **moral**
There are plenty of
things to say to calm
a hopping mad
Grasshopper Mother.
"I don't know" is not
one of them. }

frog's new shoes

Frog was watching TV one afternoon when he saw this great commercial for new skateboard shoes. The guy in the commercial puts on the new shoes, then 360 kickflips a kerb, fakie ollies a rubbish bin, and rides a nosegrind into the sunset.

Frog ran right out and got the shoes.

He laced them up and jumped on his board.
He tried the 360 kickflip and wiped out.
He tried the fakie ollie and smashed into the rubbish bin. He tried the nosegrind and spread himself on the pavement.

Cat skated over and helped him up.

"Nice shoes," said Cat.

"Thanks," said Frog.

[moral Everyone knows frogs can't skateboard, but it's kind of sad that they believe everything they see on TV.]

deer, mouse, rabbit, & squid

Deer, Mouse, Rabbit, and Squid sat on the steps trying to decide what to do.

"Let's go see a movie," said Deer.

"Great," said Mouse.

"Great," said Rabbit.

"There's nothing good on," said Squid.

"Let's play Frisbee in the park," said Mouse.

"Great," said Rabbit.

"Great," said Deer.

"My tentacles are too tired," said Squid.

"Let's go shopping," said Rabbit.

"Great," said Deer.

"Great," said Mouse.

"That's so boring," said Squid. "I'm just going to go home."

And she oozed off down the street.
Deer, Mouse, and Rabbit looked at each other.

"Great," they said. Then they ran off to see a movie, play Frisbee in the park, and go shopping.

[**moral** Squids will be squids.]

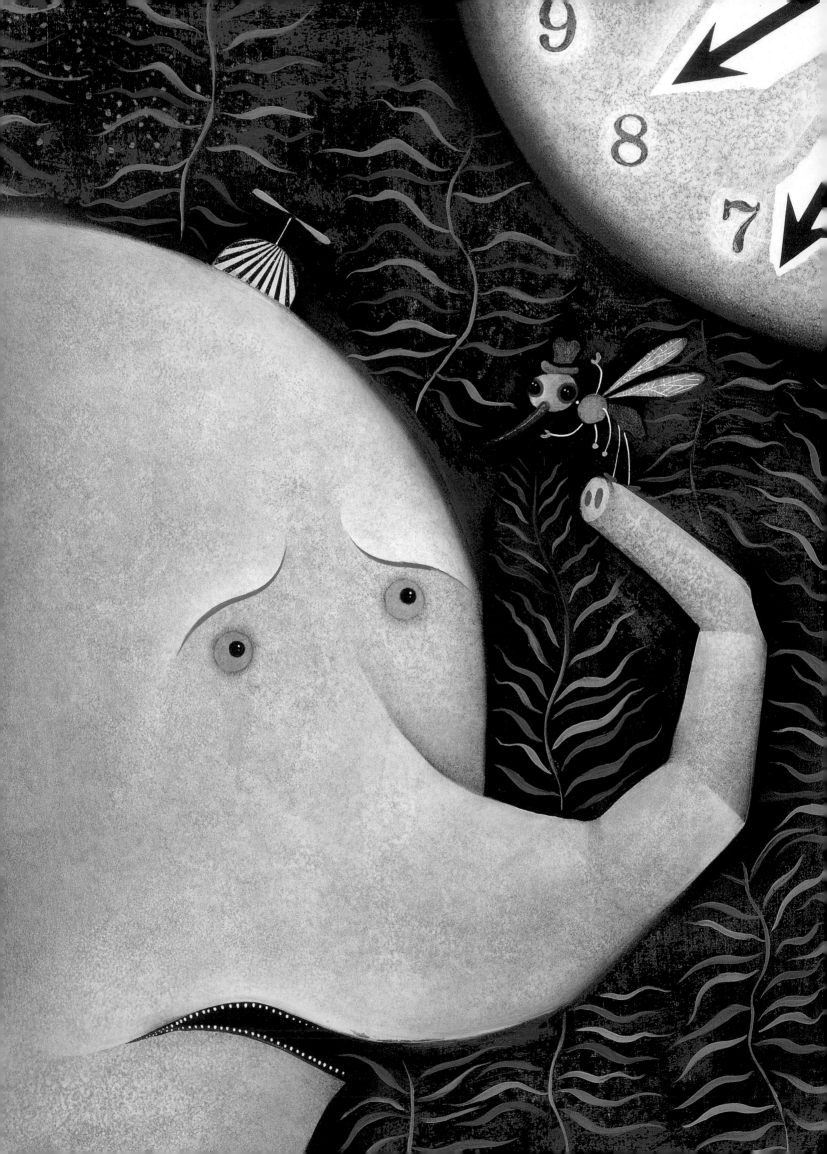

elephant & mosquito

Elephant and Mosquito stayed out late one night and completely lost track of time.

"Oh no," said Elephant, when he finally saw a clock. "I was supposed to be home twenty minutes ago. My parents are going to kill me. I'd better call home now."

"Ah, why bother?" said Mosquito. "You'll be home in five minutes. What's the big deal?"

So Elephant didn't call.

When he got home, his parents grounded him for a week because he didn't call to say he was going to be late.

{moral}
Don't ever listen to a talking bug.

he who . . .

Skunk, Musk Ox, and Cabbage were sitting around the front porch at Skunk's house.

Slowly but surely,
the porch filled with
a terrible smell.

"**Whoa!**" said Skunk. "Is that you, Musk Ox?"

Musk Ox shook his shaggy head.
"No way, Skunk. That's Cabbage."

"**Uh uh,**" said Cabbage.
"That's not me."

Musk Ox and Cabbage looked back at Skunk, who suddenly became very interested in tying his shoe.

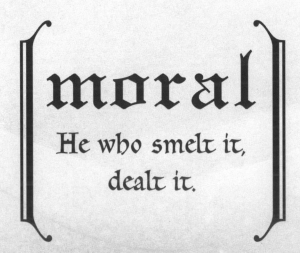

{moral}
He who smelt it,
dealt it.

rock, paper, scissors

Rock, Paper, and Scissors were assigned to be partners for the big end-of-the-year Science project.

Rock thought up the idea for the project.

Paper drew all of the charts and graphs and illustrations.

Scissors did the research and the presentation.

It wasn't a very good project, and they didn't work very hard on it, so they got a low mark.

"You should have done more research,"

said Rock, hitting Scissors.

"You should have drawn more illustrations,"

said Scissors, cutting Paper.

"You should have thought of a better idea,"

said Paper, covering Rock

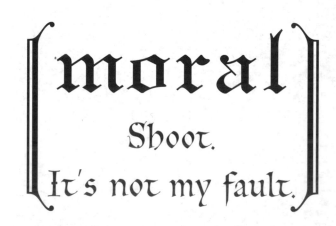

[moral]

Shoot.

It's not my fault.

pigeon pie

Pigeon was a very good artist.
But she had one very annoying habit.

Every time she finished a painting she
would show it and say, "It's not very
good" – just to get someone to say,
"Oh no, Pigeon. That's very good."

One day, after she had chased everyone else
away with her annoying habit, she showed
her painting to Sabre-toothed Tiger.

"Oh, look at my painting," said
Pigeon. "It's not very good."

Sabre-toothed Tiger licked
his long sabre teeth.

"Oh no, Pigeon. That's very good. I'm sure it will be perfect roasted or fried or even baked in a pie."

Pigeon was puzzled.
She had painted a sad-eyed clown.

Then she noticed Sabre-toothed Tiger wasn't looking at the painting.

But it was too late and . . .
the end of this fable is too messy even to tell.

[**moral**]
Whatever looks like a pigeon
and acts like a pigeon usually
makes good pigeon pie.

straw & matches

It was the end of summer vacation. Straw had done everything he could think of. He was bored. So he went over to play with someone he had been warned to stay away from.

"Let's play draughts," said Straw.

"OK I'm the red ones I get to move first I get two moves and you get one," said Matches.

"Forget it," said Straw. "Let's play ping-pong instead."

"OK I get the good paddle you stand on that side I get to serve first and you have to close one eye," said Matches.

"Never mind," said Straw. "Maybe we should just watch TV."

"OK you sit over there on the floor I'll sit on the couch I get the remote and we have to watch my choice of video," said Matches.

"I think I hear my mother calling," said Straw.
"I'd better go."

[moral Don't play with matches.]

little walrus

Little Walrus's mother told her **always to tell the truth.**

One day the phone rang.

Little Walrus was the only one home, so she answered it.

"Hello," said Little Walrus.

"Hello, Little Walrus," said Whale. "Is your mother home?"

"No," said Little Walrus. "She's out having the hair taken off her lip."

moral

You should always tell the truth.
But if your mother is out having
the hair taken off her lip, you might
want to forget a few of the details.

elephant & flea

As Elephant grew older, he also grew more responsible. One day, he and Flea went to see a movie. They liked it so much that they saw it again and completely lost track of time.

"**Oh no,**" said Elephant when he checked his watch. "I was supposed to meet Rhinoceros ten minutes ago. She is going to be furious. Do you have some money so I can call?"

Flea checked his pockets.
"Nope. Spent everything on popcorn."

So Elephant didn't call.

When Elephant finally showed up at Rhinoceros's house, he was twenty minutes late, and she was furious.

"You could at least have called," said Rhinoceros.

[**moral**
Elephants never forget,
except sometimes.]

termite, ant, & echidna

Termite and Ant had known each other since they were little. They hung out and played and ate lunch together every day.

Then one day Echidna moved into the neighbourhood.

"I come from Australia," said Echidna.

"How exotic," said Ant.

"My family name is Tachyglossidae," said Echidna.

"Let's be best friends," said Ant.

Then Ant ignored Termite and played with Echidna the whole morning. At lunchtime Ant took out her sandwich and juice.

Echidna extended her long sticky tongue and slurped up a wiggling string of ants.

"Ulp," said Ant.

{ **moral**
If you are an ant and are going to dump your best friend for a new one, you should know that Echidna is another name for Spiny Anteater. }

horseshoe crab & blowfish

Horseshoe Crab and Blowfish were always fighting.
They would use any excuse to start a fight or to keep one going.
One day Horseshoe Crab accidentally bumped Blowfish.

"Watch where you're going, fossil face," said Blowfish.
"Who are you calling fossil face, balloon brain?"
said Horseshoe Crab.

"You're a real thickhead," said Blowfish.

"You're a real wobble bag," said Horseshoe Crab.

"Dog breath."
"Pea-brain."
"Bozo."
"Dumbo."

Horseshoe Crab and Blowfish called each other every name
they could think of. Finally, one year later, neither one could
think of another bad name.

"Spanking head," said Horseshoe Crab.
"Spanking head?" said Blowfish.
"What's a spanking head?"
"I don't know," said Horseshoe Crab.

"Then you are
a . . . erh . . . uh . . .
spanking head too,"
said Blowfish.

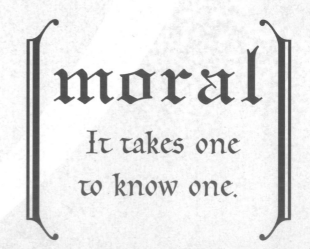

[moral
It takes one
to know one.]

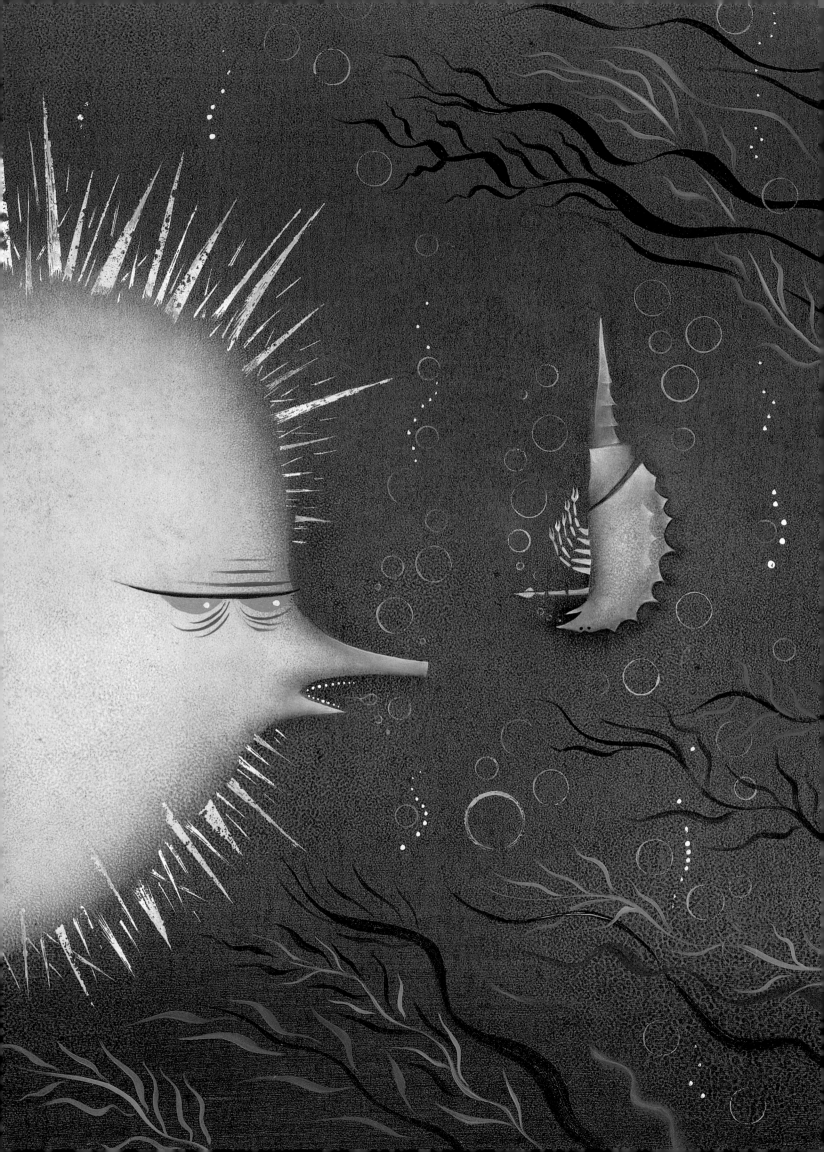

piece of toast
& froot loops

Piece of Toast and Froot Loops sat on the breakfast table, arguing over who was loved the most.

"Of course everyone loves toast the most," said Piece of Toast. "I'm half of 'eggs and toast' and all the toast in French toast. I am the toast with the most. Who could not love me?"

"We'll soon find out," said Froot Loops. "Because I am a good source of eleven essential vitamins and minerals containing 20% of the minimum daily requirement of Vitamin C, Iron, Thiamin, Riboflavin, Niacin, Vitamin B6, Folate, Vitamin B12, and Zinc (based on a 2000-calorie-a-day diet and a one-cup serving size not including the milk). I also have one gram of dietary fibre per serving and fifteen grams of sugar, yellow dye #6, blue #1 and #2, and red #40. BHT has been added to preserve freshness . . ."

But while Froot Loops was rattling off his nutrition facts, Mum had a cup of tea, Dad drank coffee, Son ate a doughnut, and Daughter said she'd get a bagel on the way to school.

Toast got cold and stiff, and Froot Loops got very soggy.

[moral] Breakfast is the most important meal of the day.

slug's big moment

Slug was interested in only one thing – herself. She was so busy thinking about herself, she never learned anything.

Worm tried to help Slug in History class by asking her, "What two countries were in the Spanish-American War?"

Slug looked up from the note she was writing to herself. "Huh?"

Snail tried to help Slug in Science class by asking her, "What colour is the great blue whale?" Slug looked up from her name that she was doodling in her notebook. "Huh?"

Then one day Larva saw a chance to help Slug change her ways.

"Slug, what is that big thing behind you that looks like a steamroller?" asked Larva.

Slug didn't look up from the friendship bracelet she was making for herself.

And the last thing she said was, "Huh?"

[moral Slugs are not unlike Squids.]

hand, foot, & tongue

One evening at dinner, Hand, Foot, and Tongue got into a heated argument over who had the toughest job.

"I have the toughest job," said Hand.

"Every day I work from sunup to sundown. I button shirts. I tie shoes. I hold the spoon and fork to feed all of us. I have to be strong enough to punch with a fist, and gentle enough to pat a baby. I definitely have the toughest job."

"No you don't," said Foot. "I have the toughest job.

"Every day I have to carry all of you. And I'm not complaining or anything, but I usually have to do it in the dark – stuck in a smelly sock and laced in a shoe. I have the toughest job."

Then Tongue spoke up.

"I am a fleshy muscular organ attached to the floor of the mouth. I help in both speech and taste. I start the process of digestion by moving food into position to get ripped and mashed and crushed and smashed to little bits by the teeth. Then I cover the little food bits with saliva and shape them into slimy blobs of guck that I push down the throat and – "

"That's sick," said Hand.

"Disgusting," said Foot.

[**moral** There are some things we don't talk about at the dinner table.]

duckbilled platypus vs. beefsnakstik®

 "I have a bill like a duck and a tail like a beaver," bragged Duckbilled Platypus.

"So what?" said BeefSnakStik®. "I have beef, soy protein concentrate, and dextrose."

"I also have webbed feet and fur," said Duckbilled Platypus.

 "Who cares?" said BeefSnakStik®. "I also have smoke flavouring, sodium erythorbate, and sodium nitrite."

"I am one of only two mammals in the world that lay eggs," said Duckbilled Platypus.

"Big deal," said BeefSnakStik®. "I have beef lips."

{moral

Just because you have a lot of stuff, don't think you're so special.

elephant & gnat

In his later years, Old Elephant became a wise and gentle creature. One night he and Gnat stayed out late and completely lost track of time.

"Oh no," said Old Elephant when he finally saw a clock. "I was supposed to be home an hour ago. I'd better call home now."

"Why bother?" said Gnat. "Mrs Elephant is surely sleeping, and you'll just wake her up if you call."

So Old Elephant didn't call.

When he got home, Mrs Elephant was furious. And she never forgot.

[**moral** Don't forget the other moral about bugs, and always, always, always call home.]

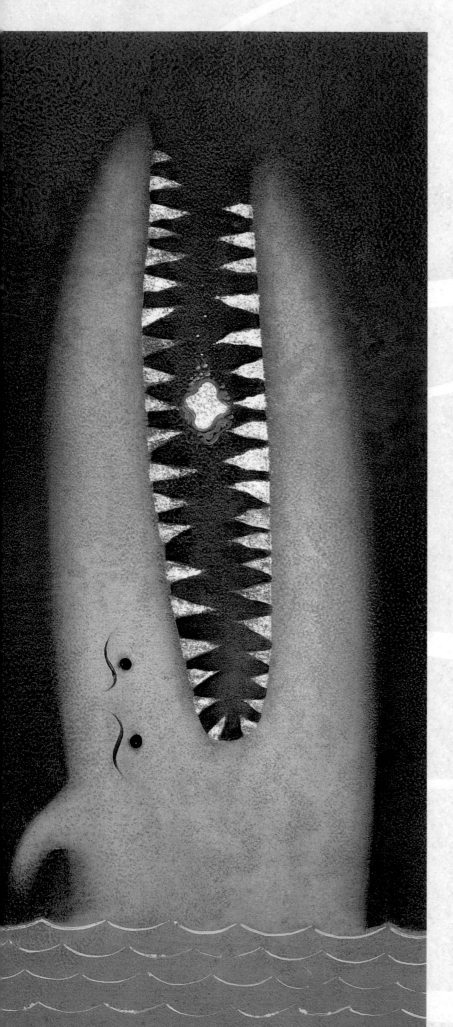

Shark, Wasp, and Bacteria ate lunch together every day.

"No one else ever sits with us," said Shark, ripping into his tuna sandwich with his double row of huge razor-sharp teeth. "What's their problem?"

"It's just not fair," said Bacteria, infecting her pudding. "Why won't anyone give us a chance?"

"We're just misunderstood," said Wasp, stabbing his pizza and injecting it again and again and again with paralyzing venom.

mo

Think

ral

about it.

You have just finished reading fables about all kinds of bossy, sneaky, funny, annoying, dim-bulb people . . . I mean *animals*.

"What fun," you are thinking.

"I should write some of those myself," you are thinking.

But before you get started, it just occurred to me that you might want to know one more little bit about Aesop.

Aesop used to tell this one fable about a really bossy creep "Lion" who ruled a city. When the really bossy creep guy who ruled Aesop's city heard this fable, he didn't like it.

So he had Aesop thrown off a cliff.

{ **moral** }
If you are planning to write
fables, don't forget to change
the people into animals *and*
avoid places with high cliffs.

VIKING/PUFFIN

Published by the Penguin Group
Penguin Books Ltd, 27 Wrights Lane, London W8 5TZ, England
Penguin Putnam Inc., 375 Hudson Street, New York, New York 10014, USA
Penguin Books Australia Ltd, Ringwood, Victoria, Australia
Penguin Books Canada Ltd, 10 Alcorn Avenue, Toronto, Ontario, Canada M4V 3B2
Penguin Books (NZ) Ltd, Private Bag 102902, NSMC, Auckland, New Zealand

Penguin Books Ltd, Registered Offices: Harmondsworth, Middlesex, England

First published in the USA by Viking, a member of Penguin Putnam Books for Young Readers, 1998
Published in Great Britain by Viking 1998
10 9 8 7 6 5 4 3 2 1

Published in Puffin Books 1999
10 9 8 7 6 5 4 3 2

Text copyright © Jon Scieszka, 1998
Illustrations copyright © Lane Smith, 1998

Design: Molly Leach, New York, New York

All the paintings in this book are actually illustrations.

No animals were hurt in the renaming of these fables.

And yes, we know that "squid" is often thought of as the preferred form for the plural of
"squid". But if "squids" is good enough for the *Encyclopaedia Britannica*, it's good enough
for us. And it's funnier too.
Moral: Simon says, "Don't forget to read the fine print."

Filmset in Janson, Francesca Gothic and Fette Fraktur

Made and printed in Italy by Printer Trento Srl

British Library Cataloguing in Publication Data
A CIP catalogue record for this book is available from the British Library

ISBN 0–670–88227–5 Hardback
ISBN 0–140–56523–X Paperback